a ladybird

a giraffe

# Using this book

Ladybird's *talkabouts* are ideal for encouraging children to talk about what they see. Bold colourful pictures and simple questions help to develop early learning skills – such as matching, counting and detailed observation.

Look at this book with your child. First talk about the pictures yourself, and point out things to look at. Let your child take her* time. With encouragement, she will start to join in, talking about the familiar things in the pictures. Help her to count objects, to look for things that match, and to talk about what is going on in the picture stories.

*To avoid the clumsy use of he/she, the child is referred to as 'she', **talkabouts** are suitable for both boys and girls.

Published by Ladybird Books Ltd
80 Strand London WC2R ORL
A Penguin Company

1 3 5 7 9 10 8 6 4 2

© LADYBIRD BOOKS MMIII

Printed in Italy

# talkabout
# Wild animals

written by Lorraine Horsley
illustrated by Alex Ayliffe

All kinds of animals big and small...
Who do you think is...
the tallest?
the biggest?
the smallest?
the longest?

7

How many...

spots does the ladybird have?

tails does the tiger have?

ears does the monkey have?

legs does the spider have?

Fur and feathers, scales and shells...
What is each animal covered in?

What would these animals feel like
if you stroked them?

Five little speckled frogs...
Tell the story.

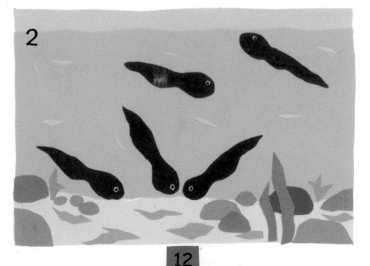

Look at these animals.
How do they move?

How many different ways can
you move?

Can you match these animals to their shadows?

Down in the jungle what can you see?
Someone is roaring, who can it be?

SNAP!

HISSSS

Can you make any animal noises?

# Find another...

elephant

panda

parrot

Who has stripes? Who has spots?

What colours can you see?

# Where do these animals have their homes?

What animals can you see?
How many babies do they have?

27

Down at the bottom of the deep blue sea, animals are hiding. Can you find...